ROB McRORY

Sandra Ann Horn

Illustrated by Bee Willey

MACDONALD YOUNG BOOKS

Rory McRory was born in a rockpool,
near the lighthouse on Faraway Point.
His mother Calypso smiled in her mirror
and combed her long green hair.
Seadog, his father, sent up a signal:

It's a bouncing boy!

All his brothers and sisters cheered, except the smallest one.
"There are too many people in this pool already," she said.

Visitors came from near and far, deep
and shallow, to see the brand-new boy;
even the wild white horses of the sea.

"What a fine young lad!" they cried.
"You can have him if you like,"
said the smallest sister.

When the visitors had gone and the pool was quiet,

Rory began to *roar*.

Calypso whistled
up the wind to sing
a lullaby;
Rory *hollered*.

Seadog gave him
jollop for the colic;
Rory *screeched*.

His brothers and sisters brought him pearls and corals; Rory *howled*.

The smallest sister went to sit on a rock all by herself and listen to the seagulls call.
" 'Qua-qua-quah!' is better than 'Wah-wah-WAH!' " said the smallest sister.

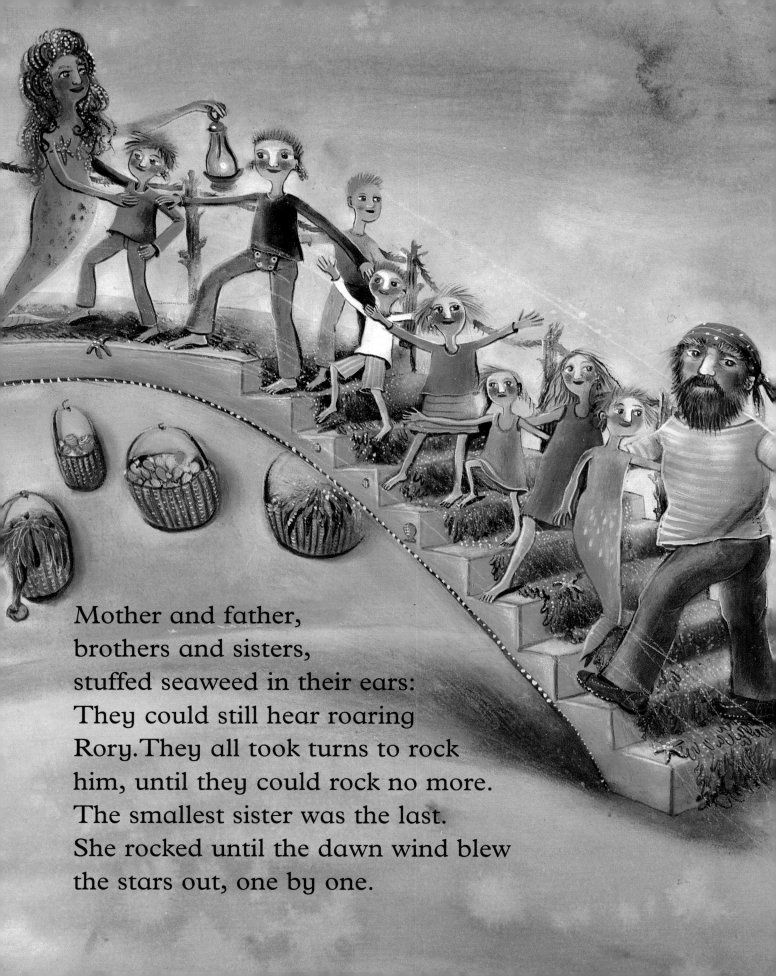

Mother and father,
brothers and sisters,
stuffed seaweed in their ears:
They could still hear roaring
Rory. They all took turns to rock
him, until they could rock no more.
The smallest sister was the last.
She rocked until the dawn wind blew
the stars out, one by one.

Rory closed one eye.
Hushhhhhh!
Was he going to sleep?
He closed the other eye.
Mother and father,
brothers and sisters,
tiptoed off to bed.

But the dawn wind blew
harder and louder.
Whooshhhh!
It stirred the sea into the foam.
Smooshhh! Smooshhh!
The white storm-horses pranced
across the waves, with manes flying
and hooves a-thunder.
Brooshhhh! Brooshhhh! Brooshhhh!

"Oh hush, you white horses!" said the
smallest sister. "You'll wake the baby up!
If he cries, I'm not going to rock him."
The horses thundered on.
Rory woke up.

Oh no!
First he hiccuped, then he
sneezed, then he began to howl.
The smallest sister stamped her foot.
"Now look what you've done!" she called.
The horses reared and tossed their foamy manes.

"Come here this minute and get the baby back to sleep!" she shouted. The horses jumped out of the sea and into the lighthouse!
"Oh!" said the smallest sister.
"I didn't really mean it."

The horses rocked the cradle
with their silky noses.
Rory yelled.
They picked the cradle up
and bounced it.
Rory howled.
"Do be careful, won't you?"
said the smallest sister.

The horses put their sleek white heads
together and whispered to each other.
Then up, out of the window and away
they flew, taking Rory with them.
Rory forgot to roar, he was so surprised.

So was the smallest sister. "Help!
I didn't mean it!" she said, but the
horses and Rory were far away,
swooping over the misty morning sea.

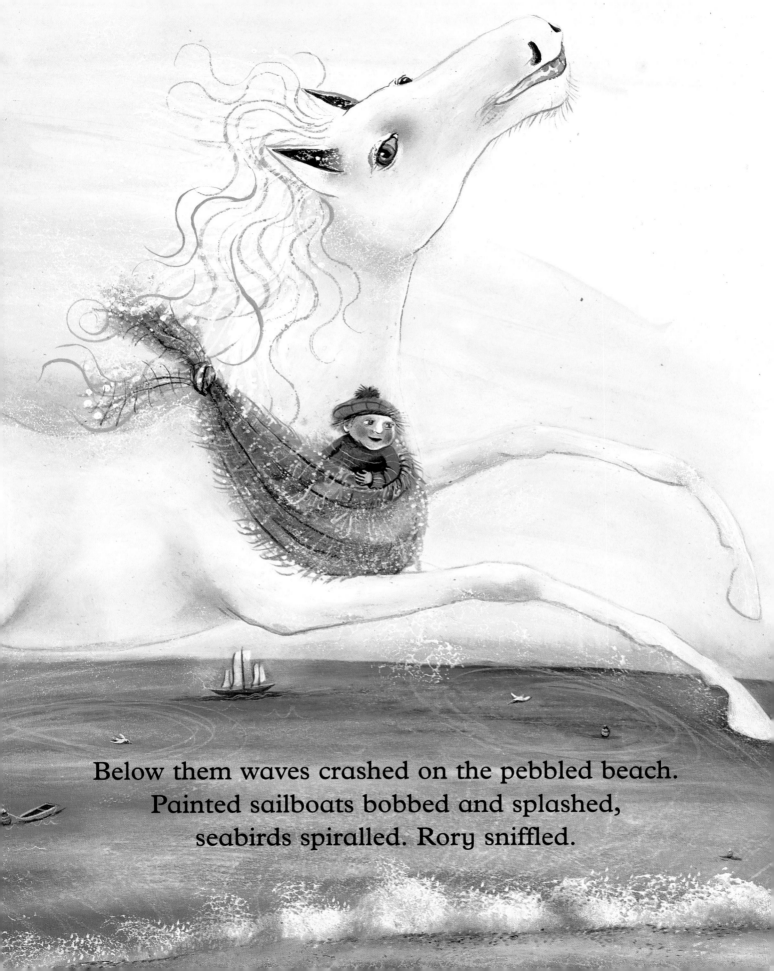

Below them waves crashed on the pebbled beach.
Painted sailboats bobbed and splashed,
seabirds spiralled. Rory sniffled.

Over the
noonday land
they went,
under the
burning sun.

One horse picked a palm leaf
to make a shady hat.
Far below, the rain forest
bustled and quivered;
hoopoes hooped and howler
monkeys howled.
They made more noise than Rory.
He put his hands over his ears.

They bumped along a raincloud
over a bustling town.
Umbrellas clashed and battled,
children jumped in puddles,
roofs glistened, gutters gurgled.
So did Rory.

The horses galloped south.
Deserts shimmered, lizards slithered,
caravans of camels swayed and moaned,
cool oases beckoned.
Rory clapped his hands.

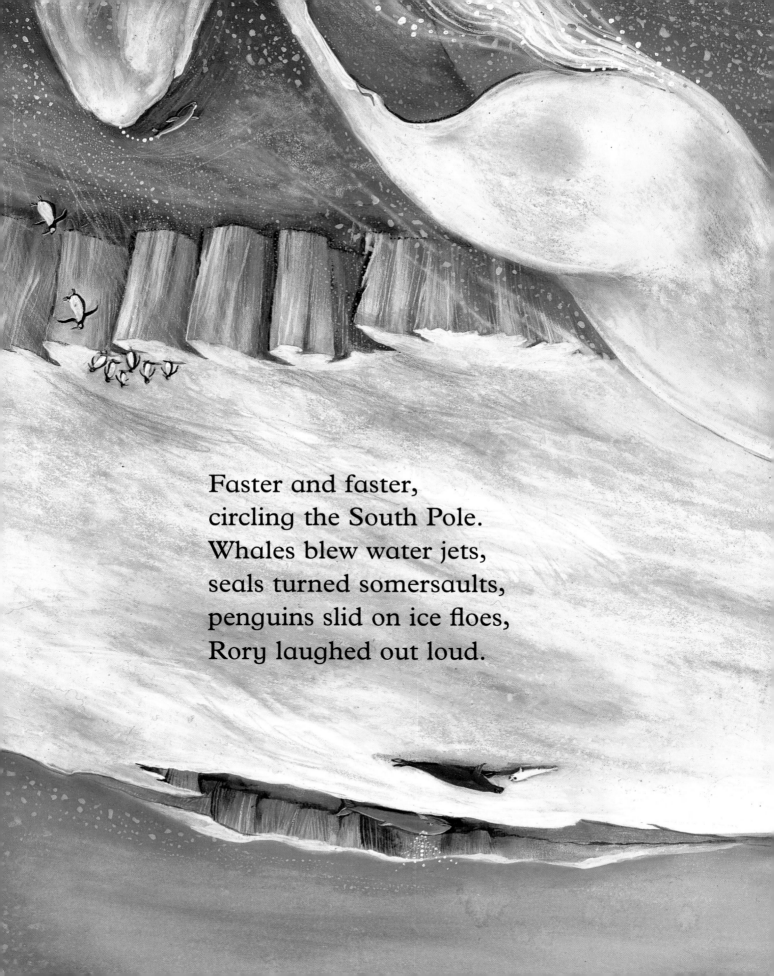

Faster and faster,
circling the South Pole.
Whales blew water jets,
seals turned somersaults,
penguins slid on ice floes,
Rory laughed out loud.

On into evening.
Owls called and foxes slunk;
valleys hung deep and shadowy,
ink-black rivers foamed round
boulders, lights came on,
cows plodded home.
Rory nodded his head.

Into the friendly night,
under the welcoming stars,
round and round a quarter moon,
past Betelgeuse and Vega,
Orion and Cassiopeia, through a
comet's orange fiery tail.

Through half-closed
eyes Rory watched the
moon set behind the sea
and the sun come rolling up,
spreading a golden path across the
waves, meeting the lighthouse beam.

The horses leapt in through the window
with a salty splash and put Rory in his cradle.
The smallest sister had watched day and
night for Rory to come home.
She was so glad to see him.
And...

... Rory was not roaring.
He was smiling in his sleep!
Rainclouds and deserts and
stars filled his head, sunset
and shadows danced
in his eyes.
Rory, the peacefullest
baby in the wide world.

"You're my Snory McRory!" said the smallest sister. Then she kissed him very gently on his nose, so as not to wake him up.

For Eliot, with love – S.A.H.

Text copyright © 1998 Sandra Ann Horn
Illustrations copyright © 1998 Bee Willey

First published in Great Britain in 1998 by
Macdonald Young Books
an imprint of Wayland Publishers Ltd
61 Western Road
Hove
East Sussex
BN3 1JD

Printed and bound in Belgium by Proost International Book Co.

British Library Cataloguing in Publication Data available.

ISBN: 0 7500 2505 0